To Mike, Heather & baby Bradley
with love from Kay

February 2007

I Love You
As Much...

I Love You As Much...

BY LAURA KRAUSS MELMED

ILLUSTRATED BY HENRI SORENSEN

HARPERCOLLINSPUBLISHERS

Library of Congress Cataloging-in-Publication Data
Melmed, Laura Krauss
I love you as much—/ by Laura Krauss Melmed ; Illustrated by Henri Sorensen.
p. cm.
Summary: A variety of mothers tell their children how much they love them.
ISBN 0-688-11718-X — ISBN 0-688-11719-8 (lib. bdg.) — ISBN 0-06-000202-6 (pbk.)
[1. Mother and child—Fiction. 2. Animals—Fiction. 3. Stories in rhyme.] I. Sorensen, Henri, ill. II. Title.
PZ8.3M55155Iad 1993
92-27677
[E]—dc20
CIP
AC

❖

for Michael
—L.K.M.

to Eschen and Marlene
—H.S.

Said the mother horse to her child,
"I love you as much as a warm summer breeze."

said the mother bear to her child,
"I love you as much as the forest has trees."

Said the mother camel to her child,
"I love you as much as the desert is dry."

Said the mother goose to her child,
"I love you as much as the endless blue sky."

said the mother sheep to her child,
"I love you as much as the grass on the hill."

Said the mother mouse to her child,
"I love you as much as the grain in the mill."

said the mother goat to her child,
"I love you as much as the mountain is steep."

said the mother whale to her child,
"I love you as much as the ocean is deep."

Now sleep, child of mine, while the stars shine above—
I love you as much as a mother can love.

right mindfulness
   (always keeping heaven in one's
   heart),
and right concentration
   (focusing on peace).
The Buddha taught meditations that purified body, speech, and mind. The power of his ultimate peace was so great that even wild animals were tamed.

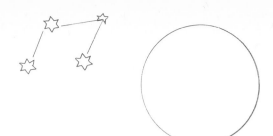

The Buddha's teachings spread throughout the land, and soon he had hundreds of followers. The disciples came from every level of society: rich and poor, man and woman, king and peasant.

In time the Buddha returned, as he had promised, to teach the Truth to King Bimbisara. The king offered the Buddha and his disciples the Bamboo Grove, which became the site of the first Buddhist monastery.

But the Buddha and his followers moved often from place to place so that they would not become attached to anything. Temples, books, and statues were not needed to follow the Buddha's path to enlightenment, for the way was found in the heart.

In one of the villages to which the Buddha traveled, there was a young woman who had been driven mad by the death of her child. She wandered from house to house, begging people to heal the child, but they could not. Finally a monk advised the woman to consult the Buddha, and so she brought the dead child to him. The Buddha looked at her with great compassion and said, "To heal your child I need a mustard seed from a home where death has never entered."

The woman went to every house in the village, but there were none that death had not visited. Then she began to understand the law of life on earth: Death is universal, and grief cannot bring back the dead. At peace, the woman buried her child and returned to the Buddha to learn the path that leads to understanding life over death.

King Suddodana wished to see his son, and so the Buddha returned to Kapilavastu with his disciples. The king still hoped that his son would succeed him to the throne. But when he saw the Buddha begging in the streets, as holy men do, he became alarmed.

The king went to his son and said, "You are a prince. It is not fitting that you should beg in the streets of your own kingdom!"

"Father, yours is the custom of kings," the Buddha replied. "But I come from a long line of Buddhas, whose custom has always been to beg for food."

The Buddha realized nothing less than a miraculous display would soften his father's heart. So he created for himself a body of lights and rose into the air to sit upon a lotus throne. King Suddodana, finally recognizing his son's holiness, fell to the ground. The people of the kingdom were moved by the Buddha, and many left the palace to follow him, including his wife, Yasodhara, and his son, Rahula.

The Buddha's miraculous powers angered one person: his cousin, Devadatta. He too joined the disciples, but he was more jealous than ever of his cousin. He offered to manage the Buddha's disciples, but the Buddha recognized Devadatta's evil nature and refused.

Enraged, Devadatta hired thirty-one criminals to kill the Buddha. But they were so affected by the great man's loving kindness that they could not raise a hand against him, and became disciples instead.

Devadatta then set loose a crazed elephant that raged down the street where the Buddha was begging for food. But the power of the Buddha's peace and love calmed and tamed the heart of the beast.

At last Devadatta decided to kill the Buddha himself. He waited at the edge of a precipice that overlooked a path where the Buddha often walked. When Devadatta saw him approach, he pushed a huge boulder over the edge of the cliff. The rock did not touch the great man, but broke into tiny pieces that flew by him. One fragment, however, cut the Buddha's foot. Devadatta had broken the law which states, "Anyone who harms a Buddha will die a violent death."

At that moment the ground split open. Flames licked Devadatta's body and pulled him to the lowest hell.

The Buddha often used parables to teach the Truth to his disciples. Two of his most famous parables are "The Blind Men and the Elephant" and "The Burning House."

The Blind Men and the Elephant

"Seven blind men were presented with an elephant. Each man felt a different part of the elephant's body: One felt the head, another the trunk, and the others felt an ear, a tusk, a foot, the back, and the tail. When asked if they now knew what an elephant was, the one at the head said, 'It is just like a pot.' The one at the ear disagreed, 'No, it is like a basket.' The man at the tusk said, 'A plowshare'; the one at the trunk said, 'A plow.' The man who knew only the foot said, 'A pillar'; the man on the back, 'A barrel'; and the man at the tail, 'A broom.'

"Those who disagree about the nature of life and death are like these blind men: each knowing a part of the Truth, but not the whole."

The Burning House

"Once there was a man who had many children. While he was away one day, his house caught fire with the children still inside. Smoke and flames encircled the house when he returned. 'Run out the door!' he cried. But the children did not realize that they were in danger and continued to play.

"Suddenly the father thought of a way to lure them outside. 'I have new toys for you to play with!' he shouted. 'A deer cart, a goat cart, and an ox cart. Who wants to ride in them first?' A moment later, the children ran safely through the door.

"The world is like a burning house. People are trapped inside, unaware of the flames of petty, worldly desires that threaten to destroy them. I am like the father who spoke to his children in a way they understood, to lead them to safety. And so I speak to you, to show you the path to enlightenment."

At the age of eighty, after preaching for forty-five years, the Buddha knew the exact moment his body would die. He would enter nirvana, a state of eternal peace where there is no more birth or death.

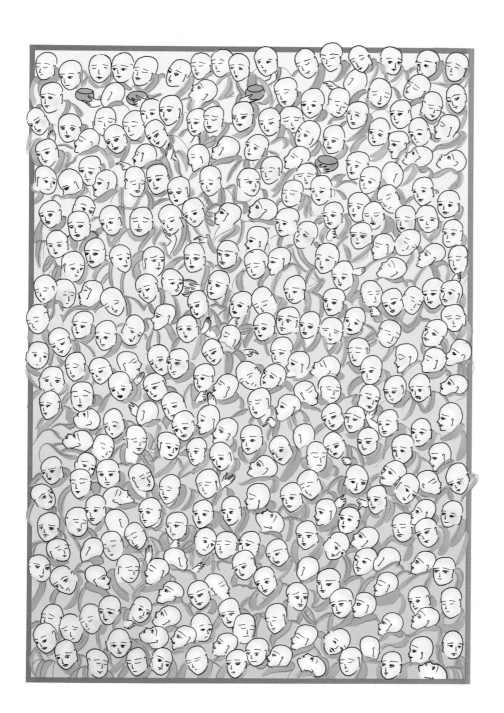

The Buddha lay down and for the last time gathered his followers around him and said:

"Remember, you must be your own light. The Truth is your light and your refuge in this world. Within your own body, the world and the beginning of the world and the end of the world are to be found, together with the way that leads to heaven. With this light, you can lead yourself to heaven."